DreamWorks

PUSS IN BOOTS
THE LAST WISH

THE PURR-FECT ACTIVITY BOOK!

BY TERRANCE CRAWFORD

Andrews McMeel
PUBLISHING®

Andrews McMeel Publishing
a division of Andrews McMeel Universal
1130 Walnut Street, Kansas City, Missouri 64106

www.andrewsmcmeel.com

22 23 24 25 26 RLP 10 9 8 7 6 5 4 3 2 1

ISBN: 978-1-5248-7756-9

Made by: Shenzhen Reliance Printing Co., Ltd
Address and location of manufacturer:
25 Longshan Industrial Zone, Nanling,
Longgang District, Shenzhen, China, 518114

1st printing—4/25/2022

ATTENTION: SCHOOLS AND BUSINESSES

Andrews McMeel books are available at quantity discounts with
bulk purchase for educational, business, or sales promotional use.
For information, please e-mail the Andrews McMeel Publishing
Special Sales Department: specialsales@amuniversal.com.

Throughout the years, Puss has been known by many names: DIABLO GATO, THE FURRY LOVER, CHUPACABRA, FRISKIE TWO-TIMES, and the GINGER HITMAN. But to most people, he's PUSS IN BOOTS — outlaw, lover, fighter, and a cat on a mission.

In this activity book, you'll go on an adventure with Puss and his unlikely comrades. So grab a pen, pencil, or whatever writing tool you'd like (but leave the swords to Puss, those tricky weapons will tear the pages!) and get going.

DON'T FORGET TO INTRODUCE YOURSELF TO PUSS!

NAME: _____

_____

BIRTHDAY: _____

IF I HAD A CATCHPHRASE, IT WOULD BE: _____

_____

MY FAVORITE PAIR OF SHOES IS: _____

One of Puss's favorite things to do is dance. If it's a dance fight, then he'll Tuesday-Night-Dance-Fight you forever.

Write a song for Puss to dance to.

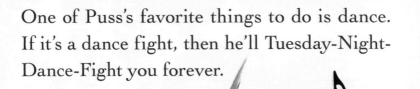

_____

_____

_____

_____

_____

_____

_____

_____

_____

_____

_____

_____

_____

Puss goes by many other names. Do you have any nicknames? Who gave them to you? If you don't have any nicknames, are there ones that you wish you had? Write all about them!

_____

_____

_____

_____

_____

_____

_____

_____

_____

_____

_____

_____

_____

_____

_____

Long ago, THE WISHING STAR fell and landed in a mysterious dark forest and was hidden at its center. The Wishing Star promises to grant one wish to whoever can find it.

If you could only wish for one thing, what would it be? Endless riches? True love? Eternal life? In the space below, write what you would wish for and why. Then draw it out!

A ___ + Wishing
Star

Three cheers for PUSS IN BOOTS! He's the thief who steals only hearts. And money. And maybe sometimes art. Add to Puss's collection by drawing a portrait in the frame.

Puss's latest adventure involves a surprising number of fireworks. Create your own fireworks display below! Draw to your heart's content and let your imagination soar!

Of course, not everyone who meets Puss is happy to see him . . . like the town's governor, who crashes Puss's party. Help Puss escape the governor by navigating him through the maze below.

If you need help, flip to page 93.

The governor's knickers are in a twist! Design
a pattern for them below.

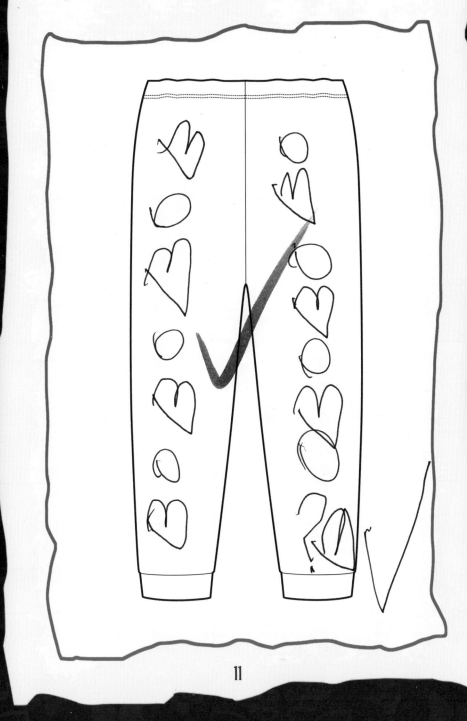

One of Puss's iconic weapons is his sword. Using the grids below, draw Puss's sword.

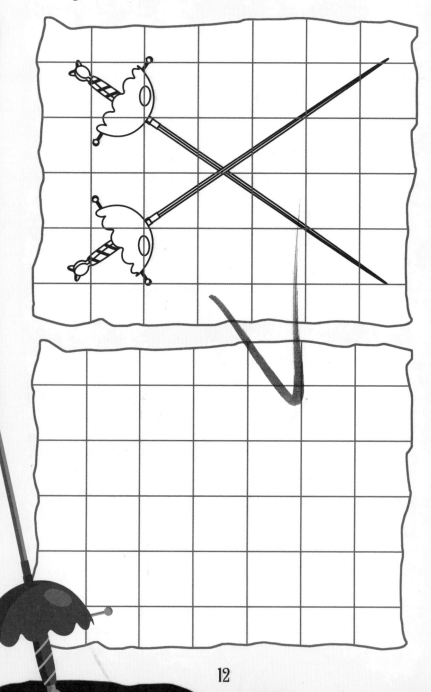

All cats have nine lives, and Puss has just learned that he's on his last one. That means it's time for retirement—according to the vet (who is also a barber, and maybe even a comedian).

What are nine things that you want to accomplish in life? Maybe it's a visit to Machu Picchu, or maybe it's inventing a new flavor of ice cream. Write nine goals below!

1. _____

2. _____

3. _____

4. _____

5. _____

6. _____

7. _____

8. _____

9. _____

Unfortunately, Puss leaves his sword behind after a run-in with a dangerous wolf. Have you ever lost something? Did you find it, or did you learn to live without it? Write about it below!

Puss takes refuge with Mama Luna. Mama Luna tends to many cats. At her house, Puss is given the name "Pickles."

IF A NEW CAT SHOWED UP AT YOUR DOORSTEP, WHAT WOULD YOU NAME THEM?

_____

DO YOU HAVE ANY OTHER PETS? HOW WOULD THEY FEEL?

_____

_____

_____

_____

HOW WOULD YOU PLAY WITH THE CAT?

_____

_____

_____

_____

_____

_____

_____

A good outlaw always has a good backup plan. Even as a cat burglar, you never know when things are going to get . . . *hairy*. Come up with a secret identity and backstory to use in a pinch if you ever get caught. You never know when they might come in handy!

MY SECRET IDENTITY'S NAME IS: _____

_____

_____

MY BACKSTORY: _____

_____

_____

_____

_____

_____

_____

_____

_____

_____

_____

_____

Meowing is only Puss's third language. Help him out by giving the off-screen cats something fun to say.

X P I L B O E C D D S I F W R
B X F K M L O F L Z F P H W T
C T A D H L I C T V N M R C B
B P J S L R H T Z A N U Y A N
T P U A Y T A Z T S L Y V B Y
R R R B H B M W C E C O U C H
B S B K O O I R O A R B N X J
C D A M G T A C R R R Z X E M
S L W O B T M A R V W A C B S
D R S E C L N T J E Y K Y T Y
E A S H Z E T N K B T S Y C O
G W E R B B V I N N L A T O T
E R S S T E F P D U K S W N C
W H A P A O O D M F A K S O U
I B P D S L M T E V L J M G E

Mama Luna has a *lot* of cats. Help her locate all her kitties' things in the word search above! If you need help, flip to page 93.

Key:

BOTTLE   TOYS   SCRATCHER   COUCH

CATNIP   BOWLS   WATER   SPRAY

LITTER   COLLARS   BRUSH

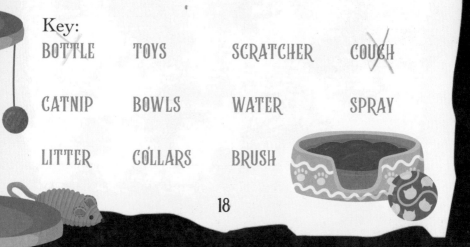

18

The Wolf isn't the only one on Puss's tail. Meet
Goldilocks and the Three Bears. They may not
look like it, but they're a family. Who do you
consider your family? Write about them below!

Goldi has her own way of doing things—
including finding Puss!

Draw a squiggly line through the set of footprints
that are *too small*. Draw a straight line through
the set of footprints that are **TOO BIG**
Circle the set of footprints that are just right.
If you need help, flip to page 93!

Imagine that you're fixing up a bowl of porridge for Baby Bear. Check off your answers below and then draw it!

MY PORRIDGE IS SERVED IN:
☐ A GLASS BOWL   ☐ AN ICE CREAM CONE
☐ A HOLLOWED-OUT TREE STUMP   ☐ A COZY MUG
☐ NOTHING! SLURP WITH YOUR PAWS

SWIRLED WITH:
☐ WHIPPED CREAM ☐ BROWN SUGAR
☐ CARAMEL   ☐ HONEY   ☐ CANDY   ☐ FLOSS

IT'S TOPPED WITH:
☐ BANANAS   ☐ CINNAMON   ☐ CHERRIES
☐ DATES   ☐ WALNUTS

IF I WERE TO SERVE THIS AT A RESTAURANT, I'D NAME THE RESTAURANT: _____

_____

At Mama Luna's, Puss grew a beard. But now he wants it shaved off! Imagine that you're Puss's barber. Draw some facial hair for him in any way you'd please. Maybe you'd like to give him a **BIG** mustache— or maybe a shiny goatee!

Also at Mama Luna's, Puss meets a dog, Perrito.
Using the grid below, draw Perrito!

Perrito wants to be a therapy dog and comfort those who need it. But perhaps we could all use a little therapy—or some extra help! Think about a time that you went to someone for help. Maybe it was a therapist, or maybe it was a friend for assistance on math homework. Then write about it below!

_____
_____
_____
_____
_____
_____
_____
_____
_____
_____
_____
_____
_____
_____
_____
_____
_____

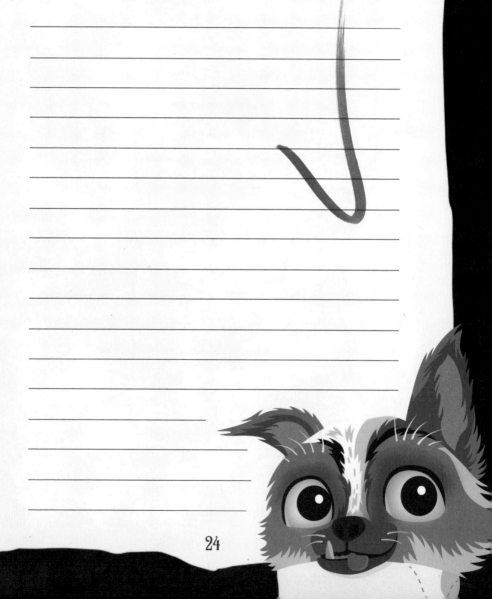

Jack Horner runs a pie factory! Imagine that you're making up your own kind of pie. It can be as goofy as you'd like! Write the recipe for your pie below.

INGREDIENTS:

_____

_____

_____

_____

DIRECTIONS:

_____

_____

_____

_____

_____

_____

_____

_____

_____

Hey, *you!* You're on pie packing duty. Help Horner's pies get ready for shipment by drawing a line to SIX different pairs of identical pies.

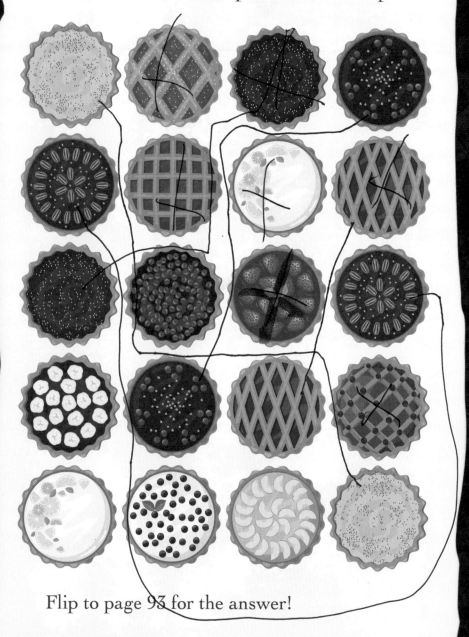

Flip to page 93 for the answer!

In Jack Horner's trophy room, Puss runs into his old comrade Kitty Softpaws.

Imagine that you can run into someone special. Maybe it's an old friend, a former teacher, or even a favorite celebrity! What would you say to them? Write about it below!

THE PERSON I'D MOST LIKE TO RUN INTO IS:

_____

_____

WHAT I'D SAY TO THEM IS: _____

_____

_____

_____

_____

WHAT I'D LIKE TO ASK IS:

_____

_____

_____

_____

_____

_____

With so many people out for Puss, it was bound to be a real *catfight* when they all caught up! Use the calamity to escape Jack Horner's unscathed. This is an escape, so you'll have to work your way out from the middle!

Flip to page 93 for the answer!

Like most dogs, Perrito loves to dig. What secrets do you think lie beneath our heroes' feet? Is it buried treasure? Dinosaur bones? A mysterious riddle? Draw your answer below!

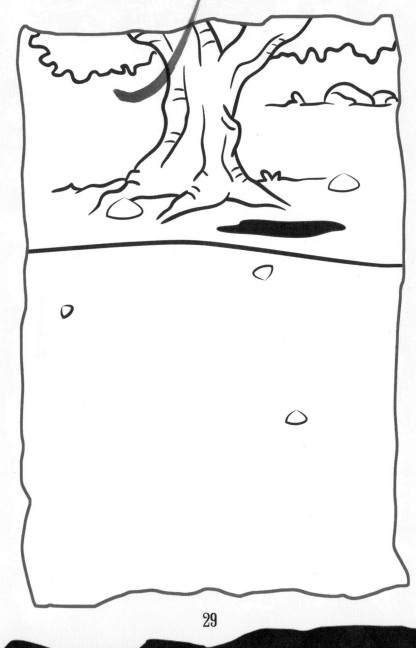

Fill out the activity below for a fun rhyme!

The _____ is _____ and
           PLACE   ADJECTIVE

far, within its _____ you'll
                    NOUN

_____ the star. A single wish
       VERB

burns _____ and bright, this
           ADJECTIVE

map's the _____ so hold on tight!
                 NOUN

When Puss, Perrito, and Kitty enter the mysterious dark forest, they discover the map changes depending on the person holding it.

What is the scariest thing you can imagine traveling through? Maybe it's a dark trail with no light, or maybe it's a sea of slime! Write what your scariest trail would be and why in the lines below.

_____

_____

_____

_____

_____

_____

_____

_____

_____

_____

_____

_____

_____

Draw your own treasure map that is specific to you. You can use landmarks that only you would know, reference inside jokes, even write it in your own special language. Just remember that X marks the spot!

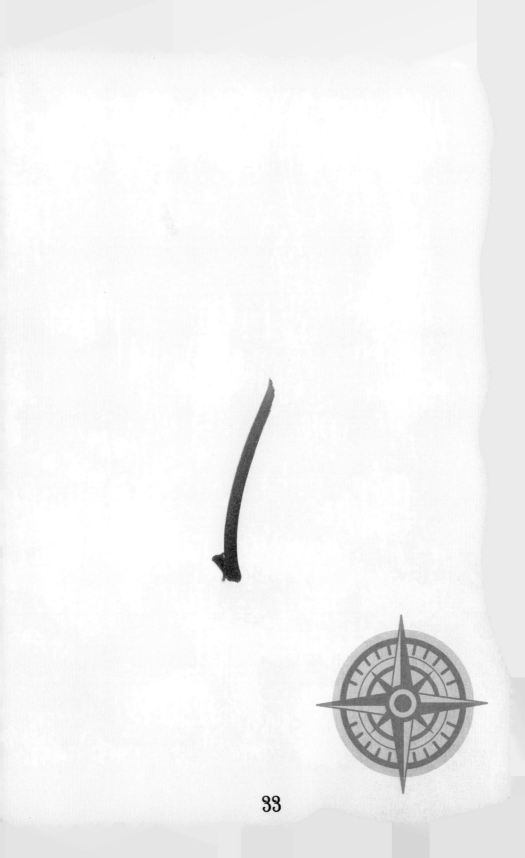

Part of Perrito's trail is wandering through a field of posies.

WHAT'S YOUR FAVORITE FLOWER?

_____

_____

_____

DRAW YOUR FAVORITE FLOWER BELOW!

When Goldi takes hold of the map, it changes to her own path and she comes across the Bears' house created by the forest's magic.

What does home mean to you? Is it your bedroom, the beach, or maybe the structure you live in? Draw your answer below!

On Puss's path in the mysterious dark forest, he comes across his own past lives. They are all very handsome, but Puss no longer connects with them like he used to.

Imagine that you're having a meeting with yourself from a year ago. What would you tell them? Write your answer below!

_____

_____

_____

_____

_____

_____

_____

_____

_____

_____

_____

_____

_____

_____

_____

_____

_____

Everyone is looking for Puss in Boots! He has the map to the Wishing Star, and everyone wants that wish. Track Puss in Boots by following the correct set of footprints.

If you need help, the answer is on page 93.

In pursuit of Puss, Jack brought a bottomless bag to bring kinds of magical items and enchanted knickknacks from his trophy room. If you had a bag that never ended, what would you keep inside? Make a list below!

1. _____

2. _____

3. _____

4. _____

5. _____

6. _____

7. _____

8. _____

9. _____

10. _____

Over their journey Puss has come to rely on Perrito and Kitty. Not quite a family, but certainly a team. Perrito proposes a group name—"TEAM FRIENDSHIP!" But Puss says that they need to workshop it.

COME UP WITH NINE IDEAS FOR TEAM NAMES BELOW!

1. _____

2. _____

3. _____

4. _____

5. _____

6. _____

7. _____

8. _____

9. _____

Puss's own song often plays in his head.

"WHO IS YOUR FAVORITE FEARLESS HERO? WHO IS BRAVE AND READY FOR TROUBLE?"

If you had a song about yourself, what would the lyrics be? Write them in below!

_____

_____

_____

_____

_____

_____

_____

_____

_____

_____

_____

_____

_____

_____

_____

_____

Wishing Star or not, there are endless ways to make your dreams come true. Write down *three* secret wishes on this page. But keep them to yourself! Everyone knows that if you say your wishes out loud, they won't come true (at least, that's what they say when wishing on a star, right?). Good luck!

1 one

2 two

3 three

In the mysterious dark forest, Puss realizes that he made Kitty feel bad awhile back, and he apologizes to her.

Apologies are very powerful. Think of a time when you did something that you weren't proud of. Did you apologize? What did you do? Write about it below. Remember: an effective apology is taking accountability for what you did!

Guide Team Friendship to reach the Wishing Star by solving the toughest maze yet.

START

FINISH

If you need help, the answer is on page 94.

Write in the English translation next to these words. If you need help, look at the images!

PERRITO _Dog_

ESTRELLA _star_

LOBO _wolf_

PAPEL _Map_

FLOR _Flowr_

MAPA _MAG MRGEK MRP_

The answers are on page 94.

Jack Horner has thirteen men, or his Baker's Dozen, to help him get to the Wishing Star.

What do you wish that you had thirteen of? Maybe it's thirteen different kinds of cookies or thirteen different pairs of boots (we don't judge!). Write your answers below!

1. _____

2. _____

3. _____

4. _____

5. _____

6. _____

7. _____

8. _____

9. _____

10. _____

11. _____

12. _____

13. _____

Of course, friends or family beat evil henchmen any day, as Puss, Kitty, and Perrito learn.

Imagine that you're putting together an all-star team of people you love. Who is on the team? Write each person's name below and why you'd include them.

_____

_____

_____

_____

_____

_____

_____

_____

_____

_____

_____

_____

_____

_____

_____

Do you know how Puss met Kitty Softpaws? That's an exciting tale . . . and all the mysteries are uncovered in the first Puss in Boots film!

Turn the page for even more activities.

When Puss was a kitten, he got his first cavalier hat. Using the grid, draw Puss and his hat.

J O A M Y K B K N S S B N D R
A X O O P Z N R R Z H O Z C A
C K I T T Y J A D M J A X I L
K T Y G S J I K G I A T L S Z
D Z D C A K Q J N B D S W Y D
F J J M N O Y A Q S K M O F T
N O I E R N L N J V Z E F D B
T D L W I M D U O D S O T S L
X E L R C X G O S E W P I I
T L A H A D I J W L C T A O L
R F L N R F T A L M S R W E Q
O M P J D G P M T O L A S P Z
J Q G X O P M A L E C H E S F
L Z P B S V F P A Z C Y C T T
O Q C S K B E A N S T A L K J

Can you find the hidden words below? If you
need help, the answers are on page 94.

Key:

BOOTS	GOOSE	BEANSTALK	MEOW
KITTY	JACK	SAN RICARDO	
SOFTPAWS	JILL	LECHE	

49

Imagine that you're making a milkshake for Puss. Check one of the following below to make him something tasty!

MILKSHAKE BASE:
- ☑ VANILLA
- ☐ CHOCOLATE
- ☐ RASBERRY
- ☐ PISTACHIO
- ☐ BANANA

SWIRLED WITH:
- ☑ CARAMEL
- ☐ CHOCOLATE SAUCE
- ☐ MARSHMALLOW FLUFF
- ☐ APRICOT PRESERVES

TOPPED WITH:
- ☐ PECANS
- ☐ BLUEBERRIES
- ☐ CHOCOLATE CHIPS
- ☑ RAINBOW SPRINKLES
- ☐ BANANA SLICES

AND ONE FINAL TOUCH:
- ☑ A CHERRY ON TOP
- ☐ CHOCOLATE SPRINKLES
- ☐ A WHOLE MUFFIN ON TOP
- ☐ BUTTERSCOTCH CHIPS
- ☐ WHIPPED CREAM

NOW DRAW YOUR CONCOCTION FOR PUSS

What is an outlaw without self-promotion?
Design your own wanted poster in the space
below! What will it look like?

Puss lost his boots. Help Puss navigate the maze and get them back!

If you need help, flip to page 94 for the answer.

Puss scores a P with his sword, a sign of his presence, wherever he goes. Use this page to design your own calling card. It can be your initials or a fun symbol, but it should be easy enough to do quickly.

Puss in Boots's name is legend. Everyone knows this daring, death-defying feline! What do you want to be known for? Think about it, then write below!

_____

_____

_____

_____

_____

_____

_____

_____

_____

_____

_____

_____

_____

_____

_____

"HUMPTY'S MIND WAS FULL OF IMAGINATION AND INVENTION." - PUSS

Use your imagination and create your own Humpty invention by drawing it in the space below. Then write in: what does it do? How does it work? It's your invention, so you get to choose!

SCRAMBLED EGGS

How many words can you make out of "Humpty Alexander Dumpty"?

HUMPTY ALEXANDER DUMPTY

_____ _____

_____ _____

_____ _____

_____ _____

_____ _____

_____ _____

_____ _____

While on a mission, Puss comes across Kitty Softpaws. She's another outlaw cat!

Kitty and Puss have a lot in common. Is there anyone you have a lot in common with, too? Maybe it's a sibling, a best friend, or even someone that you wish you knew better. Write about them below!

_____

_____

_____

_____

_____

_____

_____

_____

_____

_____

_____

_____

Humpty convinces Puss to help him steal the golden goose eggs of legend from the giant's lair! But first they must traverse through Puss's hometown of San Ricardo. Complete this maze to keep the group from getting lost.

START

FINISH

If you need help, the answer is on page 94.

What do you think that giants keep in their treasure rooms? Golden geese? Magic harps? Use the space below to draw what you think!

When the magic beans are planted, they grow to mighty heights, up to the clouds! Help Kitty, Puss, and Humpty by untangling the stalks.

If you need help, the answer is on page 94.

Everyone has treasure. For Puss, that treasure is his hat, his sword, and of course, his boots! Write in your answers below!

MY FAVORITE BOOK IS: _____
_____

A TOY I COULD NEVER GIVE UP IS: _____
_____

SOMETHING THAT WAS GIFTED TO ME IS: _____
_____

ONE OF MY FAVORITE MEMORIES WITH MY FAMILY IS:
_____
_____
_____

ONE OF MY FAVORITE MEMORIES WITH MY FRIENDS IS:
_____
_____
_____

SOMETHING THAT HOLDS A LOT OF SENTIMENTAL VALUE TO ME IS: _____
_____

J N R P O P U L R R C R O W N
G O U H L O U E U E T A X S P
D T B I Q A T H V O K W Z R U
K A Y S R W T S K K N J C J V
U Z K H E E X I C E S W W R B
F D N P R B V O N T Y O Q N L
F K I J Y C I L Z U E T J F Z
D L O G A N S T I K M V J O Z
D B A C S U L I K S X T A N J
C I B Y R S E D K I I E K U Y
X L A P Y U W V Z L B P W W L
A R J M F W E H B K I R H V M
N O F J O Z J M S W C Q L D T
A I N B M N H Y R P D N G U P
H R Q K X E D D T T Z F C A A

Puss and crew must find the treasures of the giant's castle in this wordsearch. If you need help, the answers are on page 95.

Key:

DIAMOND	COINS	SILVER	PEWTER	PLATINUM
RUBY	GOLD	JEWELS	CROWN	SILK

Puss likes to say, "To pull off this job, you must do *exactly* as I say!"

FOLLOW PUSS'S INSTRUCTIONS EXACTLY!

STEP 1. Draw a cat.
STEP 2. Add a funny hat.
STEP 3. Give the cat a cape that billows in the wind.
STEP 4. Draw the cat a speech bubble.
STEP 5. Write a joke for the cat to say!

Success! Puss has managed to steal one of the golden eggs. Did the legend mention them being so *heavy?* Help Puss make his way out of the giant's castle and back to the beanstalks!

If you need help, the answer is on page 95.

One of these coins is not like the others! Use your outlaw's intuition to figure out which of these coins is a counterfeit, or fake coin!

If you need help, the answer is on page 95.

It seems that Puss in Boots's reputation precedes him! Finish this poster using the other side as a guide.

Between Puss's blade, Kitty's stealth, and Humpty's brain, they've assembled one top-notch crew. Draw a line connecting each member to their matching icon. If you need help, flip to page 95 for the answers!

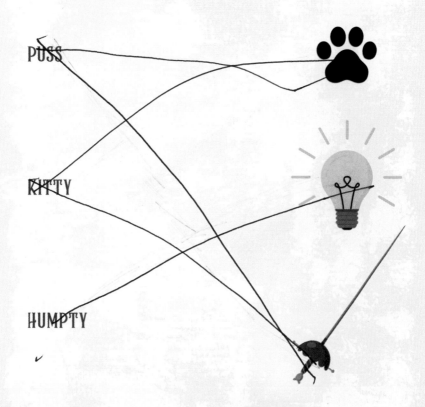

PUSS

KITTY

HUMPTY

Do you have a special skill? What is it?

_____

_____

_____

Fill in the empty speech bubble below to create your own story.

Puss might never admit it, but he needed a team to help with his mission. When was a time that you needed a team to rely on? Maybe a friend helped you out of a sticky situation? Write about it below!

Imagine that you're designing your very own treasure—a crown suitable for royalty! What is it like? Check your choices below, fill out the prompt, and then draw your crown!

MY CROWN IS MADE OF:
☐ SILVER
☐ GOLD
☐ PEWTER
☐ PAPER
☐ CANDY

IT IS:
☐ SMALL   ☐ BIG

IT IS ADORNED WITH:
☐ DIAMONDS
☐ GUMMY BEARS
☐ POM POMS
☐ RAINBOW SPRINKLES
☐ RUBIES

SOMETHING SPECIAL ABOUT MY CROWN IS THAT IT:

IT IS ALSO ADORNED WITH:
☐ PEARLS
☐ EARWAX
☐ CHOCOLATE CHIPS
☐ GLITTER
☐ AMETHYSTS

_____

It's time for the crew's big score! Unscramble the words below and use the allotted numbers to figure out the secret phrase! If you need help, flip to page 95 for the answers.

TOUBSISPSNO

Puss in Boots

SSTFAPITKYOTW

Kitty Softpaws

TYUDHYTPMUPM

Humpty Dumpty

KCAJ

Jack

IJLL

Jill

ABALSKENT

Beanstack

Big Score

A good outlaw is always prepared for anything that may come their way. What are some things that a swashbuckling adventurer should always have on them? List and draw some items below —as the giant's lair proves, the sky's the limit!

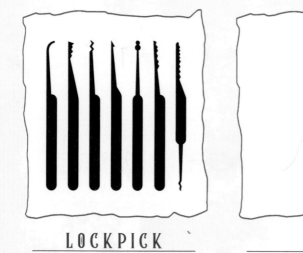

LOCKPICK

Only the messy crews leave behind proof that they were ever there! Help Puss and his gang keep a low profile by drawing a line to match their footprints.

If you need help, the answers are on page 96.

Puss would love nothing more than seeing a book about his own adventures. Design a book cover for the legend of Puss in Boots.

She's just as skilled as Puss—and, she'd argue, even better. Using the grid, draw Kitty Softpaws.

Though he had only just met her, Puss grew increasingly fond of Kitty Softpaws.

WHO IS YOUR NEWEST FRIEND?

_____
_____
_____
_____
_____

HOW LONG HAVE YOU KNOWN THEM?

_____
_____
_____
_____
_____

WHAT'S YOUR FAVORITE THING ABOUT THEM?

_____
_____
_____
_____

Puss in Boots is bilingual, which means that he is cool in two languages! Write in the English translation next to these words. If you need help, look at the images!

LECHE ___Milk___

GATO ___Cat___

SOMBRERO ___Hat___

ESPADA ___Sword___

HUEVOS ___Eggs___

GANSO ___Goose___

BOTAS ___Boots___

PATAS ___Paws___

BIGOTES ___Whiskers___

If you still need help, the answers are on page 96.

Puss's outfit is part of his legend! If you had a legendary outfit, what would it look like? Write in and fill out your answers below!

MY HAT WOULD LOOK LIKE: _____

_____

_____

MY MASK WOULD LOOK LIKE: _____

_____

_____

I WOULD WEAR:
☐ A ONESIE
☐ A DRESS
☐ A SHIRT AND PANTS
☐ OVERALLS
☐ SOMETHING ELSE

MY SHOES WOULD BE:
☐ STILETTOS
☐ SENSIBLE SNEAKERS
☐ NO SHOES!
☐ BOOTS, OF COURSE
☐ SLIPPERS

MY CAPE HAS SPECIAL EMBROIDERY ON IT. IT IS:
☐ MY CRUSH'S NAME   ☐ MY PET'S FACE
☐ MY FAVORITE QUOTE   ☐ A BANANA

I CALL MY COSTUME: _____

_____

Great job! Now imagine that you can design Puss's next disguise. What would it look like? Maybe you think he'd look better if he traded in the boots for sneakers, or the hat for a fancy bandit's mask! Go nuts, The Furry Outlaw will let you try anything *once*. Draw in your costume for Puss below.

Imagine that you're interviewing Puss for your local newspaper. What would you ask him? Think about it, then write some questions below!

_____

_____

_____

_____

_____

_____

_____

_____

_____

_____

_____

_____

_____

_____

_____

_____

_____

_____

Nothing is more adorable than a soft, innocent kitty. Except for maybe a soft, innocent, *dreaming* kitty. Use the space about Puss's head to draw what you think his dreams look like!

Without her claws, Kitty Softpaws can't pick locks as deftly as Puss can. Show her how it's done by guiding Puss's claw safely through the locking mechanism.

If you need help, flip to page 96.

Accept no *copycats!* Puss in Boots is unique. (I mean, have *you* ever met a talking cat?) Circle the *real* Puss in Boots (aka, the one with all of his accessories) amongst these imposters!

If you need help, the answer is on page 96.

Imagine that you get to decorate your very own golden egg. What would it look like? Would it have googly eyes or an intricate pattern? Design it below!

Puss likes to fiesta when he's done with a mission. Help him plan a party below by checking off one option for each item!

MY PARTY TAKES PLACE AT:
☐ NIGHT
☐ IN THE MORNING
☐ IN THE MIDDLE OF THE DAY

THE KIND OF MUSIC PLAYING IS:
☐ SALSA
☐ ROCK 'N ROLL
☐ POP MUSIC
☐ HIP HOP
☐ CLASSICAL

FOR APPETIZERS, I'M SERVING:
☐ PIGS-IN-A-BLANKET
☐ CHARCUTERIE BOARD
☐ SPINACH AND ARTICHOKE DIP
☐ SOUP
☐ BREAD AND BUTTER

FOR THE ENTREE, I'M SERVING:
- ☐ SALMON
- ☐ CHICKEN
- ☒ FILET MIGNON
- ☐ EGGPLANT PARMESAN
- ☐ ROASTED DUCK

FOR DESSERT:
- ☐ ICE CREAM SUNDAES
- ☐ FLAN
- ☐ STRAWBERRY CHEESECAKE
- ☐ FRUIT TRAY
- ☐ LECHE FRITA

ALL GUESTS GO HOME WITH A
PARTY FAVOR! I'M GIVING OUT:
- ☐ GOLD COINS
- ☐ PHOTOS OF PUSS
- ☐ SIGNED AUTOGRAPHS FROM
  PUSS, OF COURSE
- ☐ PUSS IN BOOTS CALENDARS
- ☐ MINIATURE PUSS IN BOOTS
  ACTION FIGURES

Of course, no fiesta can begin without invitations! Design an invitation for Puss's fiesta below.

What was the best fiesta that you've ever been to or read about? Think about it, then write your answer below! What made it so special? Would you want to go to a fiesta like that in the future?

_____

_____

_____

_____

_____

_____

_____

_____

_____

_____

_____

_____

_____

_____

_____

_____

_____

_____

_____

_____

_____

Puss in Boots is no housecat!

He is a globetrotting adventurer—as well as a highly regarded connoisseur of fine leche—whose exploits have taken him around the globe. Draw the places you would like to visit below and use the next page to write what kind of adventures you would have!

ANSWERS!

Flip through these pages to see the answers to the puzzles throughout the book.

PAGE 10:

PAGE 18:

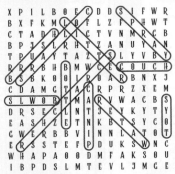

PAGE 20:

PAGE 26:

PAGE 28:

PAGE 37:

PAGE 43:

PAGE 44:

PERRITO = DOG

ESTRELLA = STAR

LOBO = WOLF

PAPEL = PAPER

FLOR = FLOWER

MAPA = MAP

PAGE 49:

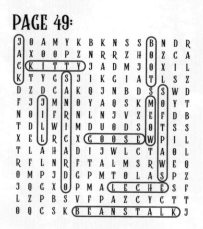

PAGE 52:

PAGE 58:

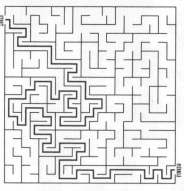

PAGE 60:

PAGE 62:

```
J N R P O P U L R R C R O W N
G O R U H L O U E U E T A X S P
D O T B Y I O A T H V O K W Z U
K A Z H E R W T S K N J C U S U
U Z K D E X I C E E S W N W R L
F D N P R B V O T T F N F L Z Z
A I A E Q A N T I T I V J N J Z
D L O G A S U L E E I S X T A A
D B A C S Y R S U S I I E K U Y
C I B Y R U I Q T I L B P W W L
X L A P P U W W E K L R H V W L
A R J M F W E J O Z B I R H C H
N O F J O I O S N S W C Q L D T
A I N B M N H Y R P D N G U P
H R Q K X E D T T Z F C A A
```

PAGE 64:

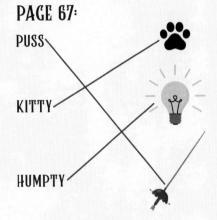

PAGE 65:

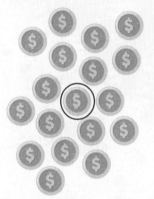

PAGE 67:

PUSS

KITTY

HUMPTY

PAGE 71:

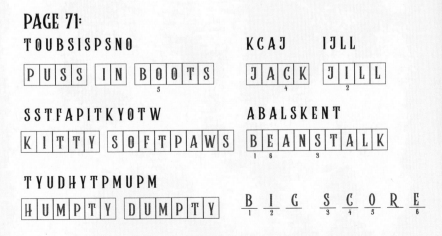

TOUBSISPSNO

P U S S | I N | B O O T S
        | | 5

SSTFAPITKYOTW

K I T T Y | S O F T P A W S

TYUDHYTPMUPM

H U M P T Y | D U M P T Y

KCAJ   IJLL

J A C K   J I L L
      4   2

ABALSKENT

B E A N S T A L K
1 6   3

B I G   S C O R E
1 2   3 4 5 6

95

PAGE 73:

PAGE 83:

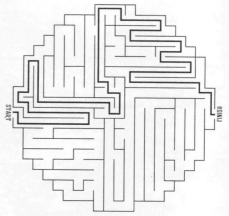

PAGE 77:

LECHE = MILK

GATO = CAT

SOMBRERO = HAT

ESPADA = SWORD

HUEVOS = EGG

GANSO = GOOSE

BOTAS = BOOTS

PATAS = PAW

BIGOTES = WHISKERS

PAGE 84: